Harold the helpful hiker

See the back pages to learn more about illustrator Daniel Pantano and writer Jeffrey Zygmont

---

for Charles Casimir
my family's Harold – J.Z.

for Jeanne and Larry
*parents who encourage
me to create* – D.P.

HELPING EDUCATE YOUR CHILD ABOUT NATURE

In nature some creatures are predators, while others are prey. We gently make that point and show relationships among animals in this fanciful children's tale about characters who subdue those basic instincts to achieve a higher goal. While depicting animal habitat and behavior, our story also demonstrates the value of cooperation. It promotes active involvement by children with the natural world and emphasizes responsible stewardship of the Earth achieved by assisting nature.

Harold's family drove to the White Mountains of New Hampshire.

His mother and father planned to go hiking with Harold.

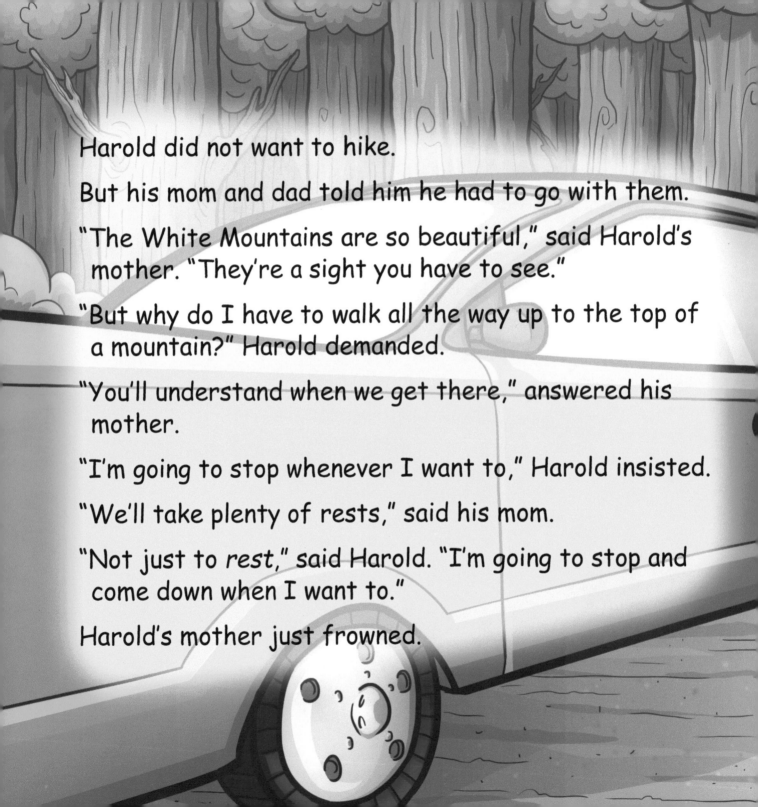

Harold did not want to hike.

But his mom and dad told him he had to go with them.

"The White Mountains are so beautiful," said Harold's mother. "They're a sight you have to see."

"But why do I have to walk all the way up to the top of a mountain?" Harold demanded.

"You'll understand when we get there," answered his mother.

"I'm going to stop whenever I want to," Harold insisted.

"We'll take plenty of rests," said his mom.

"Not just to *rest*," said Harold. "I'm going to stop and come down when I want to."

Harold's mother just frowned.

Harold emptied his backpack. He took out his school books and pencils and pens. He took out a squishy old orange from school lunch he had hid long ago in the bottom.

"Now you have room for all this," said Harold's father.

His dad handed Harold a sweater, a cap, two bottles of water, a peanut butter and jelly sandwich, and a bag filled with trail mix.

"Oh boy, trail mix," shouted Harold.

"That's for our hike," said his dad. "Now put it in your backpack with these other things."

"What?" shouted Harold. "You mean I have to carry all this stuff up the mountain?"

"You might need it," Harold's father said.

"Why can't I just leave it in the car?" Harold answered.

Harold's father
just frowned.

On the hiking trail Harold complained loudly.

"This backpack hurts my shoulders."

"This trail is too steep."

"There's too many bugs here."

"I'm tired. Can we stop now?"

"But we've only been walking six minutes," said Harold's mother. "Let's hike a little longer and then we can rest."

"I'm resting now," shouted Harold.

Harold's mom frowned. "Okay," she said.
"But just for a minute."

Harold sat down behind a rock to hide from his parents.

"What are you doing down there?" said a voice above his head. A chipmunk gazed at him from the top of the rock.

"I'm resting," said Harold. "Hey," he wondered, "how did you get up there?"

"It's easy. I climbed," the chipmunk replied.

"But you're so small," Harold said.

"But I'm still a good climber. Watch." The chipmunk scrambled down the big rock, then scrambled back up to the top.

"Wow," said Harold. "You *are* a good climber. But don't you get tired?"

"Sure I get tired," the chipmunk answered. "But it's worth it. A lot of good acorns fall on this rock from that oak tree."

Harold heard the chipmunk crunching and munching above him.

After eating an acorn, the chipmunk asked Harold, "Hey, are you going to just sit there?"

"No," Harold grumped. "My parents are making me hike up this mountain."

"Really?" marveled the chipmunk. "You're going all the way up to the top?"

"That's what my parents think," Harold answered.

"I'd love to go up to the top," said the chipmunk. "I bet that's really something to see."

"Then why don't you do it?" asked Harold. "You're such a good climber."

"But I could never climb that far," said the chipmunk. "I'm so little. Look at how short my legs are."

Harold thought for a moment. He said, "I have a sweater right here in my backpack. I'll put it on and you can ride in the pocket."

So upward they went.

The chipmunk looked out from the pocket with excitement. But Harold was starting to trudge to keep up with his parents.

"Hey," Harold suddenly shouted. "What's this icky stuff all over my face?"

"There is nothing icky about it," said a voice above him. "You simply walked into my web."

A spider dropped down on a thread and dangled in front of Harold's nose.

"But why did you make your web here?" shouted Harold. "Now it's all over my face."

"I made my web here to catch bugs for my meals," replied the spider.

"But this is a hiking trail," Harold huffed. "People walk through here."

"That is exactly why I make webs here," the spider explained. "Bugs follow people."

"I guess I never thought of that," said Harold. "I'm sorry I broke your web. But this is the trail to the top of the mountain."

"Do you say you are going to the top of the mountain?" the spider asked with excitement.

"That's what my parents say," replied Harold.

"I suppose that it must be amazing up there," said the spider.

The chipmunk called up from Harold's pocket: "They say it's an amazing sight."

"I am sure that I will never see it," the spider sighed. "I am far too small to travel that far."

Harold thought for a moment. He said to the spider, "Would you like to come along with us? I have a cap in my backpack. If I put it on my head you can ride on it."

So upward they went.

The trail became steeper and Harold grew tired. His legs hurt.

"Please do not go another step more," the spider shouted suddenly.

"But we gotta go more," the chipmunk called up from Harold's pocket. "We gotta go up to the top."

"But a bird is on that tree branch," the spider explained. "Birds eat spiders."

"But you're safe on my hat," Harold said.

"Birds flit and fly very fast," said the spider. "I do not feel safe."

The chipmunk called ahead to the bird, "Hey you there. Why don't you fly away from here. We want to walk past."

"Then just go ahead," said the bird. "I'm not blocking your way."

Harold replied to the bird, "But the spider here is afraid of you."

Harold thought for a moment. "I am a lot bigger than you," he said to the bird. "If I leave you alone will you let us walk past?"

"Of course," said the bird.

"Oh boy, oh boy," sang out the chipmunk. "We're going up to the top now."

"To the top of the mountain?" asked the bird. "I wonder what it's like up there."

"Why don't you just fly up and see?" Harold asked.

"It's too windy up there," said the bird in reply. "All the trees end and the top is just rocky and bare. The wind would blow me away."

Harold thought again. He said to the bird, "If you stand here on the top of my backpack you can look over my shoulder. Do you think you'll be safe from the wind then?"

"Oh, yes I do," said the bird.

So upward they went.

Harold walked longer and longer up the steep trail. His legs hurt.

"I'm so tired," he moaned.

The chipmunk said, "I wish I had brought an acorn along. I'm hungry."

"I'm hungry too," said the bird.

"Hey, I know," said Harold. He pulled the bag of trail mix from his backpack. He spread some on top of a rock. The chipmunk leaped out of his pocket. The bird flit down from the backpack. The chipmunk crunched and munched. The bird nibbled and pecked. Harold poured some water from his water bottle into a dent on the top of the rock. "You can have some water too," he said.

Looking ahead from above them, the spider said, "We appear to be at the place where the trees end, just like the bird described. The trail above us is rocky and bare."

Suddenly the chipmunk leaped into Harold's pocket, nestling too deep to be seen. The bird flapped to the top of the backpack.

"Hey," said Harold, "you still have some trail mix to eat."

"But look at that fox just ahead on the trail," said the chipmunk. "Foxes eat chipmunks."

The fox sat down on the trail, watching Harold and his friends.

"I'm bigger than you," shouted Harold. "So you leave this chipmunk alone."

"I don't care about the chipmunk," said the fox. "I smell something interesting inside of your backpack. I wonder what it can be."

Harold thought. "You must mean my peanut butter and jelly sandwich," he said.

"Is that what you call it?" wondered the fox. "It smells very good."

"I brought it to eat when I get to the top. My dad said I'll need it by then."

"You're hiking up to the top?" said the fox. "But you look very tired to me."

"That's why we're resting," said Harold.

"Oh," said the fox. "I see. But you still have a long way to go. I know a shortcut that will get you there faster. You won't feel as tired if you follow my shortcut."

"Don't trust him," shouted the chipmunk from deep inside Harold's pocket. "Foxes are tricky."

"Nonsense," said the fox. "I just want to make a fair trade. I'll show you my shortcut if you give me your peanut butter and jelly sandwich when we arrive at the top."

"I can watch him from over your shoulder," said the bird on the backpack. "I can make sure he doesn't try to trick us."

"I will watch him as well," said the spider from the cap.

"You have to promise to stay three steps ahead of us," Harold said to the fox. "You have to stay right where we all can see you."

So upward they went.

Harold, the chipmunk, the bird and the spider turned off the hiking trail, following close to the fox.

They followed him down into dips, up over rises, around rocky crags and through narrow slots in the rough mountainside.

But when Harold stepped around a big boulder to follow the fox, the fox wasn't there.

"Where'd he go?" said the chipmunk alarmed.

"I no longer can see him," said the spider.

"I thought he'd be waiting right here when we got around this big rock," said the bird.

"Oh, I bet you he's trying to trick us," said the chipmunk.

"Which way should I go?" wondered Harold.

Harold, the chipmunk, the bird and the spider stayed in the spot and wondered.

"I know," said the bird. "I'll fly up ahead and see if I can spot him."

"You appear to be forgetting about the wind," said the spider. "What if it blows you away?"

"I'll try it anyway," said the bird. "I'll fly up and try to find the fox."

"Make sure you look behind us," said the chipmunk. "He might be sneaking up."

"I will watch for your return from up here on the cap," said the spider.

Harold, the chipmunk and the spider waited. At last the spider cried from the cap, "The bird, the bird, I see the bird cutting back through the wind."

"I found him," said the bird. "I found the fox. He's waiting for us at the top. It's just ahead. Follow me. I'll fly ahead and show you."

"I'm sorry I rushed on ahead," said the fox when the four other hikers arrived. "I get so excited when I get near the top. I just had to run up here to see it."

Harold, the chipmunk, the spider and bird looked out at the landscape beneath them.

"I see what you mean," said the spider.

"It's a sight you just have to see," said the chipmunk.

"It's worth fighting the wind for," the bird said.

Harold said happily, "This is certainly worth a peanut butter and jelly sandwich," which he graciously gave to the fox.

THE END

JEFFREY ZYGMONT

Jeffrey Zygmont is a well regarded literary writer of prose and poetry for adults. *Harold the Helpful Hiker* is his first children's book.

Jeff describes this recent transition to children's literature as an extension of artistic literary principles to a new audience: "To reach children, I simplify the vocabulary I use, and I construct sentences that are more straightforward. But I remain just as careful about the rhythm and content of those sentences, and I choose those more-basic words with the same care about sound, syllables and meaning. I construct the story with the same concern for plot and movement, and with the same aim of involving and engaging readers, that I use in adult stories."

Consistently applying those principles to adult literature, Jeff has created books that include the poetry collections *White Mountain Poems* and *More White Mountain Poems*. His novels include *Ad Man in the Games of 2046*, *The Dropout*, and *I Am Bill Gates' Dog*. Jeff also has brought a literary sensibility to non-fiction topics, writing about computer chips and the people who finance such world-changing technologies in the books *The VC Way* and *Microchip*.

Jeff's short fiction has appeared in magazines and literary journals, and in the hardcover anthology *The Literature of Work*. As a journalist and columnist, he has contributed articles and essays to many national magazines and newspapers, writing on topics that range from automobiles and advanced technology to relationships, outdoor living and interesting people.

Jeff lives in New Hampshire. For more about him, visit jeffreyzygmont.com.

DANIEL PANTANO

As an illustrator and multi-media artist, Daniel Pantano approaches art as a means to relay his personal passion and energy to other people.

"I want to give the audience the same excitement I feel when I see the work of my favorite artists," he explains. "When I have an idea, I have to express it, and the best way to do that is to draw it."

Dan creates images using both contemporary digital methods and traditional techniques that include watercolor and acrylic painting, and charcoal and pencil sketching. To illustrate *Harold the Helpful Hiker*, Dan combined skills, including pencil drawing to create each scene and character, along with digital inking and coloring to finish the drawings, creating dynamic scenes that sparkle with allure. He utilized his abilities in character development and visual storytelling to present Harold's adventure as both an entertaining and a dramatic progression of relationships that advances from page to page.

Dan lives near Boston. He graduated with honors in fine arts and illustration from the University of Massachusetts Dartmouth. He works as a painting instructor when not producing his own art. Dan's creations include graphic novels and comics, which enable him to combine his talents to produce long works of sequential art in which his images carry a narrative.

No matter the product or the media, Dan thrives on filling blank surfaces with art. "I feel free and unstoppable," he says. "Anything can be put on a page, there are no limits or rules. It's pure freedom."

See Dan's portfolio at cargocollective.com/dpantano.

CPSIA information can be obtained
at www.ICGtesting.com
Printed in the USA
LVHW021143030319
609298LV00020B/1184/P